TEMPORADA 2009-2010

I dedicate this book to my father,
Ernani Vilela, who never loved football,
but taught me to see the art
behind every detail of life. C.V.

JANETTA OTTER-BARRY BOOKS

Photographs copyright © Caio Vilela 2014
except USA photograph copyright © Anne-Marie Weber 2014
Text copyright © Sean Taylor 2014

Original concept and photographs first published in Brazil
as *Por Onde a Bola Rola* in 2012 by Casa Amarelinha
Hardback edition first published in Great Britain in 2014 by
Frances Lincoln Children's Books,
74-77 White Lion Street,
London N1 9PF
www.franceslincoln.com

First paperback edition published in Great Britain in 2015

A catalogue record for this book is available from the
British Library.

ISBN 978-1-84780-597-3

Set in ATArta

Printed in China

9 8 7 6 5 4 3 2 1

GOAL!

FOOTBALL AROUND THE WORLD

Caio Vilela
Written by Sean Taylor

Where there's a ball... there will always be someone who wants to play football.

Brazil

Many people say the Brazilian player, Pelé, was the greatest footballer ever. He helped Brazil to win three World Cups and was so good that he once stopped a war. In 1967 his team, Santos, travelled to Nigeria to play a match. Nigeria was in the middle of a war, but the armies agreed to stop fighting so that they could see Pelé play.

When you play football, you're not allowed to use your arms and hands unless you are the goalkeeper.

But you can use all the rest of your body — your feet, your legs, your hips, your chest, your head.

USA

Football is called soccer in the US and the women's team are the stars. They won the first ever Women's World Cup in 1991, and the first women's football Olympic gold medal in 1996. Soccer is one of the most popular sports played by American children.

There are more than 6,000 different languages spoken on our planet. But children all over the world understand the language of football.

Spain

The Spanish national team played 35 matches without losing a single game, between November 2006 and June 2009. This was equal to Brazil's record for the longest unbeaten run in international football. But Spain managed something that no other national team has ever done – they won 15 games in a row.

Goals can be hard to score in a football match,
and sometimes you don't get any at all.
So when you do score a goal, it's a great feeling.

England

England has the oldest national football team in the world, along with Scotland. In 1863, a group of Englishmen formed the Football Association and wrote down the rules of modern football. But games similar to football are known to have been played in Ancient China, Ancient Greece and the Roman Empire thousands of years ago.

When a football comes your way,
you might feel excited, you might feel calm,
you might even feel a bit scared.

Playing football teaches you lots of things —
how to be quick, how to be clever,
how to see what's going on around you,
and how to be brave.

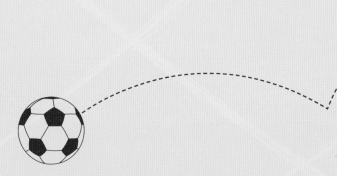

Ghana

The first-ever African professional footballer was from Ghana, whose national football team is known as the Black Stars. Arthur Wharton was born in Jamestown (now called Accra). He moved to England when he was 17, and became a brilliant sportsman. He played for Rotherham Town, Sheffield United and Sunderland.

You can play football almost anywhere —
in a garden, down an alley, in a playground,
in a park or on a beach.

Togo

The national football team in Togo is nicknamed the Sparrow Hawks. A teenager from Togo became the youngest player ever to play in a World Cup qualifier. Souleymane Mamam represented Togo in a match against Zambia when he was 13.

You don't need to buy anything
to play football. You can make a goal
out of two stones, two sticks or two shirts.

If you don't have a real football, you can make
one out of rolled-up socks, newspaper and string,
or even an orange in a plastic bag.

Tanzania

The two great rival clubs
in Tanzanian football are
Simba and Young Africans FC.
So far, these two teams have
won 36 out of 48 Tanzanian
League titles – and each club
has won the title 18 times.

Some people invent machines, some people invent medicines – and some people invent tricks with footballs.

When you trick a defender by pretending to go one way and then send them after an imaginary ball, it's called a step-over. When you throw yourself in the air and kick the ball over your head, it's called a bicycle kick.

There could be lots of new football tricks just waiting to be invented.

Jordan

On 7th June, 2013, in a Women's Asian Cup qualifier, the Jordan women's football team beat the Kuwait women's football team 21-0. One of their players, Maysa Jabarah, scored a hat-trick in an amazing three minutes.

Every football match is like a story.
It's full of characters, emotions and drama.

And no one knows how it will end
until the final whistle blows.

Iran

The greatest ever goal-scorer in international football is the Iranian, Ali Daei. Between 1993 and 2006, he played 149 times for Iran. He helped his country qualify for two World Cups, and scored 109 goals. That's way ahead of the next-highest international goal-scorer, Ferenc Puskás, who scored 84 goals for Hungary between 1945 and 1956.

There's a saying about how exciting
and surprising a game of football can be:
"The ball is round, so anything can happen!"

Pakistan

The top sport in Pakistan is cricket, and the Pakistan football team has never qualified for a World Cup, or even an Asian Cup. But that may change because, in 2011, Pakistan's Under-16 team won the South Asian Football Federation Championships.

At the end of the game you may have won, or you may have lost. But you can lose a game and still play your very best. And that's a kind of winning.

India

The highest-scoring game in the First Division of India's football league was played on 30th May 2011, when Dempo Sports Club beat Air India 14-0. Ranty Martins broke the record for goals scored in one match – he hit the back of the net six times.

Football is not about showing off how well you can play. It's about seeing how well you can play for your team.

The best players don't worry about being the star of their team. They want their team to be the star.

Nepal

Football was introduced in Nepal by young players who learnt it from other countries. It's now a very popular sport. In 2009 more than 10,000 people watched a charity match in Nepal between a team of politicians and a team of TV comedians. The comedians won 4–1.

The ball doesn't care if you're big or small.
It doesn't mind what your religion is,
what race you are, or where you are from.
It doesn't even mind if you're good at football
or not.

Anyone can play football – anywhere in the world.

China

The national football team of
The People's Republic of China
is nicknamed The Dragon or
The Great Wall. They have
won the East Asian Cup twice,
and were twice the runners-up
at the Asian Cup. Football is
very popular, and it's possible
for over 250 million people to
watch a big match on television.

You can have fun playing football
with just one friend.

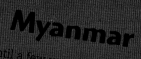

Myanmar

Until a few years ago
Myanmar, formerly known
as Burma, had an unusual
football league. All the teams
in its top league were from
the capital city, and most of
them were run by different
government departments.
The most successful club
for many years was called
"Finance and Revenue"!

No other sport brings people together like football. No other sport is played by so many people in so many different countries.

So when you are playing football you are never alone.

New Zealand

The New Zealand football team broke two records while trying to qualify for the 1982 World Cup. They travelled a record total of 55,000 miles. And they also went a record length of time without letting in a goal. Goalkeeper Richard Wilson managed nine clean sheets in a row, and that year New Zealand qualified for its first-ever World Cup.

Football Around the World

Football is played all over the world.

This map shows all the countries mentioned in this book, and the year each country's national team was founded.

USA
1913

BRAZIL
1914

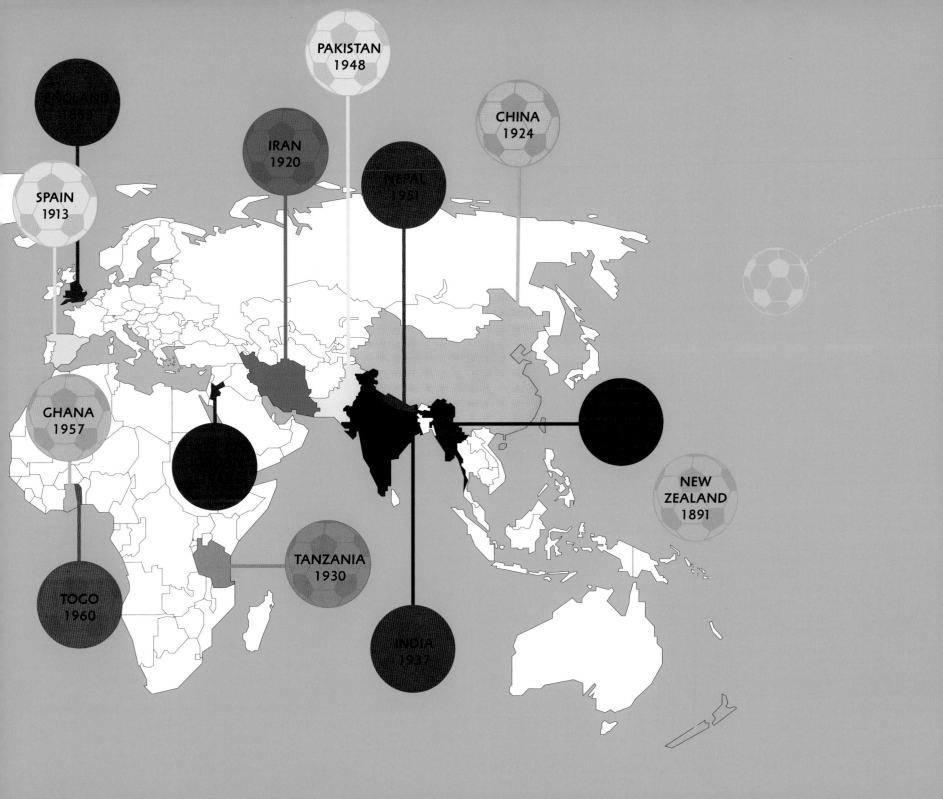

MORE WORLD-CLASS INFORMATION BOOKS PUBLISHED BY FRANCES LINCOLN CHILDREN'S BOOKS

ISBN 978-1-84780-502-7

World Alphabets:

S is for South Africa
Beverley Naidoo and Prodeepta Das

"Poetic and powerful, capturing the richness and diversity of the land and its people" – *Books for Keeps*

"A welcome addition to the highly acclaimed World Alphabets series" – *School Librarian*

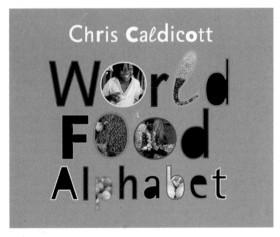

ISBN 978-1-84780-142-3

World Food Alphabet
Chris Caldecott

"A fantastically colourful look at food and its global context" – *Juno*

Frances Lincoln titles are available from all good bookshops.
You can also buy books and find out more about your favourite titles,
authors and illustrators on our website: www.franceslincoln.com